Impy
for Always

Impy
for Always

by Jackie French Koller

Illustrated by Carol Newsom

Little, Brown and Company

Boston   Toronto   London

Text copyright © 1989 by Jackie Lynn Koller
Illustrations copyright © 1989 by Carol Newsom

First Edition

Springboard Books and design is a trademark of Little, Brown
and Company (Inc.).

Library of Congress Cataloging-in-Publication Data

Koller, Jackie French.
  Impy for always / by Jackie French Koller ; illustrated by Carol
Newsom.
    p. cm. — (A Springboard book)
  Summary: Eight-year-old Impy, dismayed at the changes she
sees in her rapidly maturing twelve-year-old cousin Christina,
stubbornly tries to continue their former sharing of dolls and
funny nicknames, but Christina persists in growing up.
  ISBN 0-316-50147-6
  [1. Cousins — Fiction.]   I. Newsom, Carol, ill.   II. Title.
PZ7.K833Im 1989
[Fic] — dc19   88-29761
                                                             CIP
                                                             AC

                    10 9 8 7 6 5 4 3 2 1

                           WOR

           Published simultaneously in Canada
        by Little, Brown & Company (Canada) Limited

        PRINTED IN THE UNITED STATES OF AMERICA

To George,
who always believed

Impy
for Always

1

"Here it comes!" shouted Imogene. "Here comes the bus."

From her perch in the apple tree, she could see the big, black-windowed bus turning the corner onto her street. Imogene couldn't wait. This summer was going to be great.

"Remember, if it's not true I get my quarter back," said Clifford, still puffing from the exertion of having climbed the tree. Beads of sweat stood out on his chubby face.

"It *is* true, I told you," said Imogene. "I heard my mother say it."

"Well, I still don't believe it," said Clifford.

"Here she comes," said Imogene. "You'll see."

The bus's brakes squealed, and it came to a stop just up the street from Imogene's house. The door opened, and a young girl came down the stairs. Imogene and Clifford stared hard at her feet as she stepped from the bus.

"One . . . two . . . ," counted Clifford. "She's only got two. I told you. Give me my quarter back."

"She does not. My mother says she's got three. The other one must be growing out of her back or something."

"You're crazy!" shouted Clifford. "You're just tricking me. Nobody has three feet."

"Shhh!" whispered Imogene. "Here she comes."

The girl walked up the sidewalk and turned in at the driveway. She carried a suitcase and

4

a cosmetic case, and she looked hot and tired.

Suddenly Imogene's mother burst out of the front door, as if someone had fired her from a cannon.

"Teeny!" she shouted. "Teeny, you're here!"

Imogene's mother ran down the driveway and threw her arms around Teeny. "It's so good to see you!" she exclaimed, hugging Teeny to her, then pushing her back at arm's length again. "Let me look at you," she went on. "Oh my, your mother wasn't exaggerating a bit. You *have* grown another foot. You must be almost as tall as she is now."

Imogene felt her ears starting to burn.

"Oh," she said quietly, "that kind of foot."

Clifford started snorting. He always snorted when he laughed.

"Another foot," he shouted. (snort) (snort) "What a jerk! You thought she really grew another foot." (snort) (snort)

"Shut up," said Imogene. "Take your dumb quarter and get out of here."

6

She threw the quarter on the ground. Clifford jumped down and picked it up, then he looked up again and stuck out his tongue. Imogene pulled a little green apple off the tree and threw it at him. Clifford took off across the lawn, snorting all the way.

"Imogene, come down here," called Imogene's mother. "Come over and say hello to your cousin."

Imogene climbed down and stomped over to the driveway. She stared up at Teeny and stuck out her bottom lip.

"Boy," she said, "you sure are a disappointment."

2

Imogene sat on the edge of her double bed, watching her cousin unpack her things.

"You sure changed a lot in two years," she told her.

"So did you," said her cousin. "You were just a little bitsy thing when I saw you last. Do they still call you Impy?"

"Yup," said Imogene, crossing her eyes and making a silly face in the mirror.

"Well, don't worry. You'll grow out of it. Nobody calls me Teeny anymore."

Imogene stuck her bottom lip out again. She liked being called Impy. It was her name. Why should she grow out of it?

"Mom still calls you Teeny," she said, "and so do I."

"Well don't, because I'm not teeny anymore, as you can see, and it's silly."

Imogene stared at her. She was right about not being teeny anymore. She was almost as tall as Imogene's mom, and she was getting all lumpy and curvy like Mom, too.

"What shall I call you then?" Imogene asked.

"Christina. That's my name, isn't it?"

Imogene shook her head. "Too many dums," she said.

"What?" asked Christina.

"It has too many dums," Imogene repeated. "Like Im-o-gene, Chris-ti-na, dum-dum-dum. Too many dums."

Christina laughed. "You mean syllables,"

she said. "All right, just call me Chris then."

Imogene tilted her head and studied her cousin through squinted eyes. She didn't like people changing who they were.

"Chrissy," she compromised.

Christina shrugged. "Sounds kind of babyish, but I guess it's okay for you."

She went back to unpacking.

"Did you bring me anything?" asked Imogene.

Christina gave her a teasing look.

"Why would I bring *you* anything?"

" 'Cause you always used to."

"All right, all right, don't go sticking that lip out again," said Chrissy, laughing. "As a matter of fact, I did."

Imogene jumped off the bed.

"Is it a new Babsy doll?"

"Well, no," said Chrissy. "I'm really not into dolls anymore, Imp."

She pulled a little square package out of the suitcase and handed it to Imogene, who

10

grabbed it and quickly ripped off the paper.

"It's a book," she said, disappointment edging her voice. She opened it and looked inside. "What kind of a book is this?" she said. "It has no pictures and no words."

"It's a diary," said Christina. "You know, for writing in. It's fun."

Imogene looked up at Christina and wrinkled her nose.

"I don't think writing is very much fun," she said.

"Oh," said Christina, chuckling a little. "Well, see, it's not just for plain writing. It's for writing your innermost secret thoughts in."

Imogene tried to think of some innermost thoughts.

"You mean like about your blood and guts and stuff?" she asked.

Christina burst out laughing.

"Of course not, silly," she said. "What a weird kid you are, Impy." Then she made her

12

voice kind of soft and secret-y. "You know," she whispered, "like — about boys."

About boys? Imogene thought about Clifford sticking his tongue out and snorting like a pig. She had a few secret thoughts about him all right, but if she wrote them down her mother would probably wash her pencil out with soap or something.

"Why would anyone want to write about boys?" she asked.

Christina gave her a hopeless look.

"You'll understand," she said, "in three or four years."

Imogene shrugged and tossed the book onto her dresser.

"Want to play Babsies?" she asked.

Christina sighed. "Impy, I told you, I'm really not into dolls anymore."

Imogene flopped back down on the bed. "Well, what *are* you into?" she asked.

Christina reached over and switched Imogene's radio on, turning it up until the whole floor was shaking to the beat of the bass drums.

"Music!" she shouted, waving her arms in the air and dancing around the room.

Imogene jumped up and switched the radio off.

"Stop that!" she shouted. "You're scaring Mrs. Brisby."

"Who's Mrs. Brisby?" demanded Christina.

Imogene picked up a little silver cage and shoved it in front of Christina's nose.

"Eeeek," Christina shrieked. "It's a mouse. There's a live mouse in there!"

"I know that," said Imogene.

"Well, I'm not staying in the same room with any smelly, creepy mouse," Christina shouted.

Imogene hugged Mrs. Brisby's cage to her chest and narrowed her eyes. "Then *you'll* have to stay in the den," she said.

3

Imogene carried Mrs. Brisby's cage into the den and set it down next to the fish tank.

"There, see, you won't be lonely," she told the little mouse. "You can talk to Hotlips and Moby Dick. They're always talking."

As if to prove her right, the two goldfish glided over to the side of the tank nearest the cage and floated there, opening and closing their lips as if they were chatting away.

"Besides," Imogene continued, "it's only for a week. Until *she* goes home."

15

"Impy, lunch is ready," called her mother.

Imogene went down to the kitchen and slid sullenly into her place at the table. She was still mad at her mother for taking Christina's side about Mrs. Brisby.

"Well, are you girls having fun getting reacquainted?" her mother asked cheerfully.

"Oh yes, Aunt Irene," said Christina.

Imogene just sulked.

"What's wrong, Impy?" asked her mother.

"She's not the same anymore," said Imogene. "She doesn't even like Babsies."

"Well, Imogene," said her mother, "Christina is twelve years old now. Naturally she's changed, but I'm sure there are still things you both can enjoy. Why don't you go swimming after lunch?"

"That sounds great," said Christina.

"Yeah," said Imogene, brightening. She hurriedly finished her lunch and ran up to get her bathing suit on.

16

"Last one in is a rotten egg," she yelled from the edge of the pool in the backyard.

"Give me a break, Impy," said Christina, coming down the back steps. "I can't get in that fast." She stepped gingerly into the water. "Oh, this is freezing," she complained. With her stomach sucked in and her arms held up out of the water like a scarecrow, she waded out to a rubber raft and climbed on.

Imogene watched until she was comfortably settled, then she got a running start and made the biggest bellyflop she could right next to the raft.

"Imogene!" shouted Christina. "Don't splash."

Imogene dived down and came up under the raft and tried to tip Christina off.

"Imogene, cut that out."

"Let's play Marco Polo," said Imogene.

"Not now, Impy," said Christina. "I want to get some sun, okay?"

Imogene made a face. She grabbed the other raft and climbed on. She got up on her knees.

"Can you do this?" she asked, getting shakily to her feet. The raft slid out from under her, and she fell off and landed sideways across Christina's raft.

"Imogene, please!" shouted Christina. "Can't you play something that doesn't splash?"

Imogene slid off the raft, and Christina lay back and closed her eyes. Imogene thought of things to do that didn't make splashes. She pretended she was dead and floated facedown in the water. She pretended she was deader and let her air out and sank to the bottom. She tried to break her record for holding her breath underwater.

"Didn't you get enough sun yet?" she asked Christina when she ran out of unsplashy things to do.

There was no answer. Christina had fallen asleep.

18

Imogene sighed and stuck out her bottom lip. She looked over at the tree where her dog, Waldo, was tied. He was barking and barking. He hated being tied, but they couldn't let him loose when they were swimming because he was a Labrador retriever and he kept jumping in the water.

Imogene started to smile.

She climbed out of the pool and went over to pet Waldo. Somehow he accidentally got loose.

"Oh, Waldo, come back," Imogene called in a very tiny voice. The big dog charged across the lawn and took a flying leap into the pool. He landed right on top of Christina.

There was a great deal of barking and splashing and shrieking, and then the raft went over and Christina went under. She came up sputtering and saying naughty words.

"You shouldn't say naughty words," said Imogene.

Christina looked as if she were going to explode.

"Imogene!" she shouted. "You are a horrible little beast."

Imogene tried to look innocent. "It's not my fault Waldo got loose," she said. "But since you're all wet now, do you want to play Marco Polo?"

"No!" shouted Christina. "I do *not* want to play Marco Polo!"

4

Christina was sitting on the front porch drying her hair. Imogene was playing Babsies all by herself on the porch swing.

"You're no fun anymore," she said suddenly. "You used to be my favorite cousin."

Christina stopped toweling her hair, stared at Imogene a moment, then shook her head and smiled.

"Okay," she said, "what do you want to do?"

"Play Babsies?"

"Besides Babsies."

"Roller-skate?"

"I don't have any skates, Imp."

"Then how about bike riding? You can ride Mom's."

"Okay, let's go."

They got the bikes out and started around the block. Imogene had to pedal her bicycle very fast to keep up with Christina's big ten-speed, but she didn't mind. At last she and Christina were having fun together, just like they used to.

They rode down the steep hill and around Miller's Pond, places Imogene never got to go by herself. Then they circled up and went down Imogene's street again.

"Wait a minute," said Christina. "Let's just ride up and down here for a while."

"I want to go down the hill again," said Imogene.

"Later," said Christina. "I feel like riding here for a while."

They rode back and forth three or four times.

"This is dumb," said Imogene. "I can do this by myself anytime."

"Shhh," said Christina. "Who is that?"

"Who?" asked Imogene.

"That boy mowing the lawn over there."

Imogene looked where Christina was looking.

"Ugh!" she said. "That's Michael Radnor." She spit the words out as though they tasted bitter.

"He's cute," said Christina.

" *'Cute'?!*" repeated Imogene. "He's a slime."

Christina giggled. "He sure doesn't look like a slime," she said.

"Well, he is," Imogene insisted. "Do you know what he did? He cleaned out his cat's litter box and put the doodoo inside my Pumpkin Patch Kid's diaper."

Christina howled with laughter. "That's

hysterical," she shrieked. "I *love* it! I have *got* to meet this guy."

Imogene stared at her. "I'm going home," she said quietly.

Anyone who thought Michael Radnor was cute certainly wasn't a friend of hers.

5

Christina was taking a shower *even* though nobody said she had to, and *even* though she'd been swimming in the pool after supper and was probably clean enough already.

Imogene put on her nightgown, then she picked up the book that Christina had given her and opened it. It seemed like a book should have *something* in it. She picked up a pencil and wrote in big black letters:

TEENY ISN'T TEENY ANYMORE.

Then she closed it, put it back on the dresser, and climbed into bed. A few minutes later Christina came in and crawled in beside her. Imogene's parents came in to kiss them good night.

"You must be tired after that bus ride," Imogene's mother said to Christina.

"Boy, am I," said Christina. "I'll be asleep by the time you turn the lights off."

Imogene stuck her bottom lip out again. Christina always used to tell her ghost stories when they slept together.

"Good night, girls," said her parents as they left the room.

"Good night," answered Christina.

"Don't you want to tell ghost stories?" whispered Imogene.

Christina yawned. "Not tonight, Impy," she said. "I'm wiped out."

A few minutes later she was snoring. Imogene lay in the darkness and listened to Christina's noisy breathing for a long time.

She couldn't get to sleep. She was used to hearing the squeak of the wheel in Mrs. Brisby's cage. Mrs. Brisby always made it go as soon as the lights went out, and Imogene would make up little songs to its repetitive tune until she fell asleep.

Imogene propped herself up on one elbow and stared at Christina. She was asleep all right. Imogene slipped out of bed and tiptoed down the hall to the den.

Scritch-a-scritch, scritch-a-scritch went the wheel in Mrs. Brisby's cage. Imogene watched it going round and round. If she brought the cage back into the bedroom it might wake up Christina, and then Imogene might get punished. But it didn't seem fair for Mrs. Brisby to have to sleep in the den just because of Chrissy the Sissy.

Imogene stuck her hand into the pocket of her nightgown. It was nice and big and roomy. Plenty big enough for one little white mouse. Imogene took Mrs. Brisby out of her cage and dropped her gently into the pocket, then she padded back down the hall and climbed into bed. She lay on her back and pulled her nighty around so that Mrs. Brisby's pocket was resting comfortably on her tummy.

Mrs. Brisby scratched around inside the pocket and tickled Imogene with her tiny claws. Imogene giggled. "Good night, Mrs. Brisby," she whispered. "Sleep tight . . ."

Sometime in the middle of the night Imogene was startled awake by a loud, shrill noise. She thought at first that it was the smoke detector in the hall, then she thought it must be an earthquake because the bed was shaking so. But as soon as she was fully awake she realized that it was Christina. She was standing up on the bed screaming and hopping from one foot to the other.

Before Imogene could figure out what was happening, the lights went on and her parents rushed in. Her father was carrying a baseball bat and her mother had a can of hair spray.

Christina jumped down off the bed and kept on hopping and screaming. Imogene's parents kept running around her and shouting.

Imogene just sat and stared. It was like watching one of those old Marx Brothers movies her father loved on TV.

"What is it? What's wrong?" her parents kept shouting.

"That thing! That horrible thing!" Christina shrieked. "It was in my bed!"

"What thing?" Imogene's mother screamed, holding out her can of hair spray, as if she expected the "thing" to leap out at her at any moment.

"That . . . that mouse!" shrieked Christina.

Imogene's parents lowered their weapons and turned to give Imogene a searching look.

Imogene felt in her pocket.

"Uh-oh," she said.

"Imogene Peters!" said her mother. "I have a good mind to . . . to . . ."

Imogene's bottom lip began to quiver.

"It's not my fault," she whined. "Mrs. Brisby was lonely. She didn't want to sleep in the den. Now she's probably dead. *You* probably squished her," she accused, pointing at Christina.

Christina turned slightly green, and Imogene's father went over and gingerly pulled back the covers from the bed. He breathed a sigh of relief.

"She's not here," he said.

They started pulling the whole bed apart, and then the dressers and the closet. After half an hour the room looked like it had been hit by a cyclone, and there was still no sign of Mrs. Brisby. Imogene started to cry.

"She's gone," she whimpered. "She's gone and it's all *her* fault." She pointed at Christina again. "I hate you, Chrissy. I wish you'd go home and never come back again."

Christina looked guilty.

"Now, Impy," said her mother, "it's not

Chrissy's fault, and I'm sure you don't mean that. You're just upset. Why don't you two get your robes and slippers on, and we'll go down to the kitchen and have a snack and calm down a little."

Glumly, Imogene pulled on her robe.

"I'm sorry, Impy, really I am," said Christina. She sat down on the bed and slid her feet into her slippers. Suddenly she screamed again and kicked one of her slippers into the air. Imogene ran over and picked up the fallen slipper.

"Mrs. Brisby!" she shouted.

She reached in and pulled out a very shaken, but unharmed, little mouse.

Everyone seemed happy to see Mrs. Brisby again, even Christina.

"I'll tell you what, Impy," she said. "Why don't you go get Mrs. Brisby's cage and bring it back in here where it belongs. I think I'll feel a lot better knowing exactly where she is."

34

"Okay," said Imogene, smiling.

"Just one thing, though," said Christina. "Would you please promise to keep her *in* the cage?"

"I promise," said Imogene.

When everything was quiet and dark again, Imogene lay in her bed listening to Mrs. Brisby's wheel go around.

Scritch-a-scritch, scritch-a-scritch went the wheel. *Scritch-a-scritch-a-scritch-a-scritch.*

I love you, yes I do, sang Imogene to herself. Mrs. Brisby, I love you . . .

6

"Now, Impy," said Imogene's mother. "Daddy and I will only be gone a couple of hours. I'm sure you and Christina will have lots of fun together."

"No, we won't," said Imogene. "Chrissy is so boring. She doesn't like to do anything fun."

"Well, Christina is growing up," her mother said. "She doesn't enjoy the same things she used to, but that doesn't mean the two of you can't still be good friends. You just need time to get to know each other again. Give it a chance, okay, Imp?"

Impy scowled, but she managed a reluctant "Okay."

"That's my girl," said her mother.

Imogene followed her mother downstairs and stood with Christina at the front door until the car backed out of the driveway.

"So," said Christina, turning to Imogene, "what shall we do today?"

"We could have a wedding," said Imogene.

"A wedding?"

"Yes," said Imogene. "Babsy can be the bride and Ben can be the groom, and . . ."

"Impy," said Christina, "you have a one-track mind. Don't you like to do anything besides play Babsies?"

Imogene shrugged.

"Why don't we bake cookies?" Christina suggested.

38

"I'm not allowed to use the stove," said Imogene.

"Well, I am," said Christina. "We'll make peanut butter kisses."

"What are peanut butter kisses?" asked Imogene.

"They're peanut butter cookies with chocolate kisses on top."

They did sound yummy, but Imogene wasn't quite ready to give up her grumpy mood.

"We don't have any chocolate kisses," she said.

"Then we'll walk down to the store and get some," said Christina.

"I'm not allowed to walk to the store alone," said Imogene.

"Impy, stop being difficult. You won't be alone. You'll be with me."

"You're not a grown-up," said Imogene.

"I'm grown up enough," said Christina. "Now quit arguing and let's go."

"All right," said Imogene, "but if Mommy and Daddy yell, it's your fault."

"Nobody's going to yell," Christina insisted.

They walked over to Isaacson's Market on the next block. Christina picked out a package of chocolate kisses and started toward the register.

"Look," she whispered suddenly.

Imogene looked up from the candy display. Michael Radnor was standing in the checkout line. Imogene wrinkled up her nose.

"Would you introduce me, please, Impy?" Christina whispered urgently.

"No way," said Imogene.

"Come on. I'll buy you some Gummi Bears." Christina picked up a package and held it out.

Imogene wavered.

"And a box of Nerds?"

"Well . . . okay."

Imogene accepted the candy and walked slowly over to the checkout line. The truth was, Michael Radnor scared her to death. She tapped him timidly on the shoulder.

He turned around and stared sharply down at her.

"Hey, Imp the Shrimp," he said. "What d'you want?"

Imogene jerked her thumb quickly at Christina.

"That's my cousin Chrissy," she said. "She wants to meet you."

Christina turned bright red.

"Oh yeah?" Michael looked over at Christina, then he looked her up and down as though she had a for-sale sign around her neck and he was deciding whether to buy her or not. Finally, he grinned.

"Well, that's cool," he said. "Hi, cousin Chrissy."

Christina smiled and blushed even deeper.

"It's Christina," she said.

"Well, okay, *Christina*. What do you say we walk home together?"

"Sure," said Christina. "That'd be great."

Impy trailed behind Michael and Christina on the way home, chewing Gummi Bears and sulking. Instead of going home when he reached her driveway, Michael Radnor came up and sat on the front porch steps with Christina. Imogene sat with them for a while, but it was so boring. They just kept talking about records and movies and dumb stuff like that. Imogene yawned.

"I thought we were going to make cookies," she said.

"Later," said Christina.

Imogene scowled and picked at a broken fingernail.

"Can I use some of your nail polish then?"

"Sure, be my guest," said Christina.

Imogene sighed. Christina sure sounded happy to get rid of her. She trudged up to her room and flopped down on her bed. Tears welled up in her eyes. Outside, below her window, she could hear Michael and Chrissy

laughing. She wondered if they were laughing at her, and the thought made her face burn. Angrily, she wiped the tears away.

She got up and rummaged through the drawer where Christina kept her things. She found the bottle of nail polish and was about to close the drawer when she noticed a little blue book, just like the one Christina had given her.

Imogene lifted it out and opened it up. It was filled with writing — Christina's innermost thoughts. Imogene knew she shouldn't look in it, but there was something secretly exciting about it, like finding a buried treasure, and she kept on turning the pages. Most of the words were written in cursive, so nothing made much sense until, on the last written page, she came to a sentence that was printed in big, dark letters.

IMPY IS A LITTLE PEST!

it said.

The words struck her like a slap across the face, and sharp, angry tears stung her eyes. Imogene wanted to slap back. Down at the bottom of the page she noticed a big heart. Christina had written C. P. & M. R. in it.

Christina Peters and Michael Radnor.

Impy narrowed her eyes and stuck out her bottom lip. She folded the book back and pressed the page open, then she carried it out into the hall. She paused for a moment at the top of the stairs, then sucked in her breath, rushed down the stairs and out through the front door, and dropped the book in Michael Radnor's lap.

7

"Imogene Peters, you stink!" Christina screamed. "You just plain stink, that's all."

Christina had chased Imogene around the house, in the back door, and all the way up to her room again. Now they faced each other across the bed.

"Be quiet!" screamed Imogene. "You're scaring Mrs. Brisby."

"I don't care about your stupid old mouse. How could you? How could you embarrass me like that?" Christina's eyes filled with tears. "What did I ever do to you?"

Seeing Christina cry made Imogene feel guilty, and feeling guilty made her even madder.

"You called me a pest. I read it in your book."

"You had no business reading my book."

"It was a mistake. I just found it and it got open and I saw it — *Impy is a little pest.*"

Christina stared at her a moment, then she sniffed and wiped her tears away.

"Well . . . ," she said, "you haven't been very nice, you know."

"Well, you haven't either," Impy shouted. "Last year I waited all year for you and you didn't even come."

"I couldn't help that. I had the chicken pox."

"And then I waited a whole nuther year and now you're not Teeny anymore." Tears spilled out of Imogene's eyes and ran down her cheeks. She flopped down on the bed and sobbed. "I want Teeny back. I loved her and I miss her."

Christina stood watching a moment, then slowly the anger drained from her face and she came around and sat down on the bed next to Imogene. She reached out and smoothed back her tangled hair.

"Hey, Imp, don't cry," she said. "Come on, let's talk, okay?"

Imogene stopped sobbing, but she twisted away and buried her face in her arms and refused to look up.

"Come on, you little cornball," said Christina. "Just because I don't want to be called Teeny anymore doesn't make me a different person."

"Yes, it does," came the muffled reply.

"It does not."

Imogene looked up. "Teeny used to play Babsies and splash in the pool," she said. "And Teeny didn't like *boys*."

Christina took Imogene's arm and pulled her gently to a sitting position. She looked into her eyes and smiled.

"Hey, sure I've changed," she said. "I'm growing up. But so are you. You've changed, too."

"I have not."

"Oh, no? Why don't we go make mud pies then?"

"Mud pies? I don't make mud pies anymore. Only babies make mud pies."

"Oh, really? Well, it seems to me when I was here last we had to make about a hundred mud pies a day."

Imogene started to smile. "Not a hundred . . ."

"No, you're right. It was closer to a million."

Imogene giggled.

"See what I mean, Imp?" said Christina.

"I guess so."

"Just because I'm not Teeny anymore

doesn't really change things. There's still lots of stuff we can do together, and, no matter what, I'll always love you, *Imogene*."

Imogene smiled shyly and pulled at a piece of fuzz on her bedspread. "I'll always love you, too, *Christina,*" she said, "but . . ."

"But what?"

"But I'm *still* Impy."

Christina laughed and gave Imogene a hug. "I'm glad," she said. "I hope you'll be Impy for always."

"I will," said Imogene quickly, then she grinned and shrugged her shoulders. ". . . I think."

Christina laughed and tousled her hair.

"Come on," she said. "Let's go make cookies."

8

Making cookies was fun. Imogene got to be the candy plunker. That meant she got to plunk the chocolate kisses on top of the cookies as soon as they came out of the oven. The best part, though, was eating the mistakes. Christina said good cooks always eat all their mistakes. That's why everybody thinks they're such good cooks.

Christina knew how to do other fun things, too. She taught Imogene how to paint a rainbow on her fingernails — a different color for

every finger — and she showed her how to paint a little sparkly nail polish star on her cheek. She even showed her how to knit. Imogene knitted a little coat for Mrs. Brisby, but Mrs. Brisby chewed it up and made a nest out of it.

The rest of the week was full of "ups and downs," as Imogene's mother called them. Christina still didn't like to get splashed in the pool, and she still spent an awful lot of time riding around in front of Michael Radnor's house, *but* she did tell ghost stories, and she did play Marco Polo, and she even played Babsies once or twice. When Saturday came, Imogene had a sad spot in her tummy.

"Why do you have to go so soon?" she asked, as she sat watching Christina pack.

"Because I'm going to camp, I told you."

"But it's just as good as camp here. You can swim, and we could put up a tent in the backyard and sleep out if you want."

Christina smiled. "Thanks, Imp," she said, "but it's not quite the same."

Imogene's mouth sagged.

"C'mon," said Christina, "smile. Next year will be here before you know it, and I'll be back."

"Promise?"

"I promise. If I get the chicken pox again I'll bring them with me and give them to you."

Imogene giggled.

"That's better," said Christina. "Come on. Walk me to the bus stop."

Imogene stood beside Christina at the bus stop with her eyes squinted and her lips pressed tight together.

"What are you doing?" asked Christina.

"Wishing."

"Wishing what?"

"That the bus won't come."

Christina laughed. "I'm afraid it's not working," she said.

Imogene opened her eyes just as the bus rounded the corner. Christina bent down and kissed her on the cheek.

"Bye, Impy. I promise I'll bring you a Babsy next year."

Impy hesitated.

"Something wrong?" asked Christina.

"No," said Imogene. "It's just that, maybe you could bring me some of that sparkly nail polish instead."

Christina laughed and gave Impy a wink.

"You got it," she said.

The bus eased over to the curb and opened its doors. Christina hurried up the steps. She turned and waved. "See you next year, *Imogene*," she called out.

Imogene grinned and waved back. "See you next year," she shouted. "But *I'm still Impy!*"